THE CHRONICLES OF NED

KJP ALLEN

Dedication

Dedicated to Noah, Olga, Emmanuel, and Caleb, the family who inspired me to create this wonderful story. Time spent with each of them helped bring life to NED.

A special thanks to Rose Meza, who believed I had it in me to write children's books.

Of course, thanks to the One Above, who instilled within me the creativity and desire to bring this wonderful story to print. I give you the most credit.

NED wakes up and sits in his bed
With lots of thoughts racing around in his head.

Because he is a happy boy,
He plays quietly with his toy.

Into his bedroom, Mommy sneaks.
She pokes her head in to take a peek.

She watches him play hide-and-go-seek
Under the blanket, pretending to still be asleep.

Daddy comes in, looking for NED.
Mommy points to the blanketed outline in bed.

Daddy tickles him, wanting to play.
Mommy whispers, "Shhh," and sneaks away.

NED scampers back and forth, hiding under the blanket.

Daddy tries to catch him. "On your marks, get set!"
Daddy gives up and pretends to leave.
NED cries out, "Daddy, up, please!"

Daddy turns and asks Mommy to help, before NED can play with the new pup.
Meanwhile, Daddy leaves to test the milk to see if it is warm enough.

Mommy lifts NED into his highchair,
He begins to scream, "Pup, Pup, come here!"

Dad puts Odie in the doggie bed for NED to see
And NED drinks from his bottle hungrily.

NED finishes his milk and says, "Down, Down, Down."
It was his time to play and run around.

"Oh, no, no, no," Mommy says to him.
"Lessons first," she says with a grin.

Mommy points to the "A" and says, "Apple-Manzana."
What color, NED?"
NED says, "Apple—red."

Mommy turns the page and says, "Good boy, NED."
Quickly, he jumps down and dashes to the toy chest

and tosses all his toys, east and west. The place was a mess!

He throws the ball at his Pup, Odie, who runs to get the ball.
He chases Odie up and down the hall.

"Blue—Azul. Blue Ball!"
Ned begins screaming, "My ball, my ball!"

Mommy throws her hands up in the air and tells him, "That is all!
Yes, it is Azul Yes, Blue ball.

Now please return the toys to the chest. You made a mess."

He chooses his favorite trucks from his chest and races them on the floor
and begins crashing them into the closed door.

The faster the trucks race,
the more fun he has playing at his own pace.

He is hungry again, and calls out, "Eat, eat,"
as he climbs on the sofa to pull out his high seat.

Mommy runs in to catch him and cleans his hands and face,
as he struggles and wriggles out of her embrace.

"NED, it is time to eat. Let me strap you into your seat.
 It is time to eat your favorite treat."

He eats cucumbers and tiny sausages until he is fidgety and tired.
Which, to Mommy, means that a short nap is required.

Mommy cleans him up and sings him to sleep,
while he snuggles dreamily with his Fleecy-Plushy sheep.

"Daddy!"
Uh oh! NED is awake from his ti-dormi nap.
Daddy's free time is a wrap!

Daddy tip-toes to the door and peeks in.
NED gives a smile as he sees him.

NED yells, Daddy," as his Dad walks through the door.
Daddy says to him, "Bonjour."

He bounces up, races to and fro,
because he knows it will soon be time to go.

Each day after his nap, it is time for Odie's walk.
That means Daddy will take him to the park.

NED puts his leg over the rail,
as Odie watches and barks while wagging his tail.

Daddy grabs him and says, "Oh no you don't, my acrobat.
Let us get you cleaned up and changed, STAT."

Daddy tickles him and he tries to get away.
Daddy says, "Let us hurry and make a quick getaway."

Big Brother CK opens up the front door real neat,
and Odie jumps into NED's stroller seat.

He runs from Dad and sits in the stroller on top of Odie,
looking all mad.
He then tells Odie, "Bad, Bad."

He pulls Odie by the tail and his hair.
Odie growls and wriggles out of the chair.

Daddy says, "Odie, get out of there.
You know better."
That is NED's chair."

Big Brother CK puts Odie on his leash
to keep him out of NED's reach.

NED straps himself in the stroller while Daddy packs the treats.
Fresh fruits, yogurt, cheese, and other goodies to eat.

The trio and Odie stroll to the park, which is only a short
distance away.
Odie pulls CK every which way, barking at other dogs, and
wanting to play.

Daddy straps NED into a swing to give him a push.
All of a sudden, Odie races out from the bush.

Odie jumps up and tries to nip at NED's swinging feet.
NED ignores Odie, kicking to his own beat.

Daddy takes NED from the swing to let him sit with CK on the slide.
They both have fun as they slip and ride.

Odie jumps on the slide between them, getting in the way.
Daddy laughs at the funny display!

CK gets off the slide and takes Odie for his walk.
Daddy picks up NED and sits down to talk.

NED looks around and played with his chin
Because he wants to climb the jungle gym.

NED begins to walk to the jungle gym.
Daddy gives in and follows close behind him.

NED says, "Daddy, look! What do you see?"
Then NED races toward the tiny tree.
His feet move faster than a bumble bee.

Daddy takes off to catch him, and NED laughs as he runs.
Daddy huffs and puffs, for he is no longer a young-un.

"Slow down, NED," Daddy says.
"Wait for me, Mon Cherie"

Daddy chases NED and NED chases Daddy through the many rides,
while Big Brother CK walks with Odie close by his side"

They are all having fun, but it is time for a snack.
Daddy finds a bench to sit and eat at before they head back.

While NED begins eating his nutty puffs, the squirrels creep near.
He throws the puffs at the squirrels, clapping with cheer.

The more puffs he throws on the ground,
the more the squirrels come around.

Just then, Odie charged through, scattering all in his path,
barking loudly, exhibiting his wrath.

Odie, refreshed is happy to be back,
because he did not want to miss his share of the snacks.

"Welcome Odie," says Daddy, "Glad you are back.
Just in time, too. We were under a squirrel attack."

CK announces, "It is time to head back home.
 Mommy is there, all alone."

On the stroller ride home, NED keeps dropping his snacks.
Odie follows closely in the back.

park

home

Odie is eating all the dropped treats,
and having a grand feast, to say the least.

"Home at last," Daddy says
"Mommy will give you your supper and get you ready for bed.

Then I will tuck you in and read you a tale.
The story about Pinocchio and the Whale."

NED is all squeaky clean and ready for bed.
He is rubbing his eyes and nodding his head.

Daddy reads him a story while stroking his face, hugging him close in a warm embrace.

Daddy then whispers, "Mon fil, I love you dear,"
and gives NED his blanket and places him down with care.

After kissing him tenderly and turning off the light,
NED is in dreamland for the night.

NED's day is over and complete.
Stay tuned for more adventures of NED in his next Tweet!

About the Author

KJP Allen is a long-time educator and new writer of two prior books.

One is a book of poetry - The Beginning Journey
The other- short stories - Short Tales Unfolded
The NED series is the Third book added to her portfolio.

She now works as a Track Official and mentors students.

www.ingramcontent.com/pod-product-compliance
Lightning Source LLC
Chambersburg PA
CBHW041012170626
46815CB00003B/273